Magic Glasses

by Yogesh Patel
illustrated by Pam Adams

Published by Child's Play (International) Ltd
Swindon   New York   Toronto
© 1995 Mission   ISBN 0–85953–945–8
A catalogue reference for this book is available
from the British Library

Mr Oza and his family have moved into a shop in the High Street.

Mr Oza is an optician.

"I do hope lots of customers will come," he said. "This shop is very dirty. There is a lot to do."

"Don't worry, Dad," said the children. "We will help you clean it."

In a dusty corner, the children found a teddy bear.

"Poor old Teddy," said Malhar.
"He hasn't been looked after. Look, he hasn't any eyes."

"You have a kind voice," said Bear. "I wish I could see you."

"Our daddy will help you," said Shalini.
"He can do magic with eyes."

The children fetched the button box.
Buttons would make excellent eyes
for Bear. They chose blue ones,
but they couldn't find two the same.

Shalini sewed on the left eye.
Malhar sewed on the right eye.
"I hope it didn't hurt," said Malhar.

"Not a bit," replied Bear.
"I can see now, but not very well."

"I can see what is wrong,"
Mr Oza explained to the children.

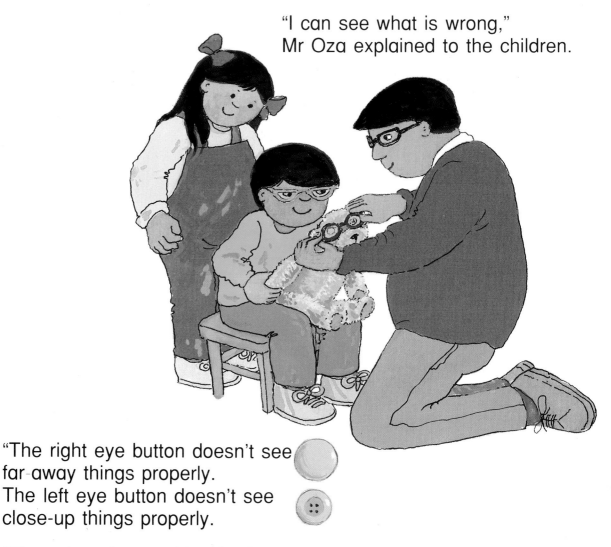

"The right eye button doesn't see
far away things properly.
The left eye button doesn't see
close-up things properly.

"There is only one thing for it.
You need glasses, Bear!

"To correct the right eye you need this concave lens.
To correct the left eye you need this convex lens."

Mr Oza tested Bear's eyes and found exactly
the right lenses. Bear chose some red frames.

Magic

"Magic!" exclaimed Bear.
"I can see clearly now.
I wish my friends
could see my new glasses."

"I know," said Mr Oza.
"We will hold
an opening party."

Mrs Oza and the children
made lots of food for the party.
They decorated the shop
with streamers and balloons.

Bear delivered the invitations
and next day all Bear's friends arrived.

"Welcome, everybody!
Please, come in!

"Let's eat first,"
suggested Mrs Oza.

Dog could smell the food.
But when he got close up
to the table he couldn't see it.

Bear had to feed him.

"You don't see close-up things
very well, Dog," said Mr Oza.
"You need glasses with convex lenses."

After they had eaten,
they played games.

"Look, I've found
some rackets," called Bear.
"Who wants to play
tennis with me?
We'll pretend there is a net."

"I do," said Rabbit.
But she couldn't see the ball
until it hit her!

Cat was umpire.
But he saw two balls at once!

"You don't see far-away things
very well, Rabbit," said Mr Oza.
"You need glasses with concave lenses."

"And you, Cat, have a turn in your eye.
One eye looks one way.
The other looks the other way.
So you see everything double."

"Now, Dog,
keep your eyes open.
I am going to shine
a light in them."

"These lenses will help to strengthen the muscle in your weaker eye, Cat. We'll have to cover the good one with a patch for a while.

"Now for the best part. I've got lots of frames for you to choose from."

When they had
finished choosing,
Mr Oza fitted
the lenses.

All the animals
had exactly
the right frames.

Now, Rabbit could hit the ball!

And Cat could keep the score.

Dog fetched the balls.

Hedgehog had an idea.

"Let's bring all
our children to have
their eyes tested.
I'm sure mine
needs glasses.
She is always losing me!"

Next day, the toys told their children
to wash their hands and brush their hair
and come with them to Mr Oza's shop.

So, they did!

"You have lots of customers now!"
said the children.

"Thanks to Bear!" said Mr Oza.

"Thanks to magic glasses!" said Bear.

The End